book

Congratula...
I hope you
David Radman
2022

"I BET A DRAGON COULD"

FOR MY GRANDSON,
KASEN DAVID EVEN

story by
David Radman

illustrations by
Douglas Shuler

There's a pet store on the corner
And they have some pets for sale
But they never have the ones I want
Like a tiger or a whale.

I always stop to see if
They are selling something good
What would make this pet store better?
Well, I bet a dragon could.

If they only had a dragon
I'd run home to get my change
Then I'd buy him in a second
I'm sure mom won't think it's strange.

I could teach him many tricks
Like how to sit or how to stay
I am sure he'd learn quite quickly
We would practice most the day.

He could help out at my birthday
There would be free dragon rides
And if he sat and sloped his back
He'd make the perfect slides.

Do you think a dragon's useful?
Do you think a dragon's good?
What could make a party better?
Well, I bet a dragon could.

He could fly us up into the sky
And maybe to the moon
But we couldn't stay there too long
Mom will have lunch ready soon.

And if I miss the bus one day
He'd fly me down to school
And everyone would see him then
And think that I was cool.

I would take my new pet dragon
To the "All Three County Fair"
And I'll bring mom's note to enter him
Into the pet show there.

PET SHOW

Then down the street we both would go
Just me and my pet dragon
I bet he'd be quite comfortable
While sitting in my wagon.

Oh, the things that I can think of
Should I tell you? Yes I should
Because, you might not be able
But I bet a dragon could...

Play many games of hide and seek
And many more of tag
I bet he'd eat potato chips
He might just eat the bag.

I'd take him to the swimming pool
And bring my swimming things
We'd want to race the other kids
And show off his large wings.

We would always win at football
He'd be tough to block I fear
And to score on playing hockey
When he's wearing all that gear.

And it's always good to have him
When the weather gets too bad
'cause he'd make the best umbrella
Anyone has ever had.

He'd be very good at board games
Quite tough to beat I'm told
But you get a lot of practice
When you're 600 years old.

He could carry all the groceries
And deliver all our mail
It's just hard to take him shopping
Clothes his size just aren't on sale.

There's a zillion things to do
If mom and dad just understood
Who could ever make me happy?
Well, I bet a dragon could.

He could help dad with the car
If he needs to change the tires
And on cold, cold nights we'd always have
The best fireplace fires.

And of course he'd help out mom too
Not one better could be found
While mom vacuums he'd lift
And move the furniture around.

Then at night when it was bedtime
And we both had brushed and flossed
We would wrestle on the floor
And then after he had lost,

Dad would tuck us into bed
Mom would kiss us both goodnight
Then bring both of us some water
Before turning out the light.

And me, under my covers
With my dragon on the floor
Would talk and laugh and giggle
'til we couldn't anymore.

Then just before we'd fall asleep
He'd tell me dragon tales
The kind with knights and castles
And big ships with bigger sails.

They would be amazing stories
And I'd want to hear much more
But would fall asleep while listening
And hope he doesn't snore.

And I know that I'll be dreaming
About how life got so good
What could make this life much better?
Well, I bet a dragon could.

THE END

ABOUT THE AUTHOR

David Radman is an award-winning author who began writing children's stories as a single father, when his two daughters were very young. His love of being a dad inspired him to share his creativity through the magic of storytelling.

His first book, *Santa's Zany, Wacky, Just Not Right Night Before Christmas*, won the gold medal Moonbeam Award in 2014, and was a finalist in the USA Best Books competition that same year. In 2018, he wrote *When Grandpa Gets Going*, and in 2019, *Peek and Boo are Looking for You*, both of which were published by Black Rose Writing.

He continues to write stories that he hopes to share in the future. David lives in Littleton, Colorado, with his wife and two Wheaton terriers.

ABOUT THE ILLUSTRATOR

Douglas Shuler has been drawing and painting for as long as he can remember. Classically trained in traditional art mediums, he transitioned to digital methods and can create imagery using most any technique. He has a passion for science fiction and fantasy illustration and has worked on everything from book covers to comic books, from video games to television concept art. Internationally published, he is best known for his fantasy illustrations that appear in the popular trading card game, Magic: The Gathering. This is his third book with David Radman

BLACK ROSE
writing™

This is a work of fiction. Names, characters, businesses, places, events and incidents are either the products of the author's imagination or used in a fictitious manner. Any resemblance to actual persons, living or dead, or actual events is purely coincidental.

ISBN: 978-1-68433-937-2
PUBLISHED BY BLACK ROSE WRITING
www.blackrosewriting.com

Printed in the United States of America
I Bet a Dragon Could is printed in Arial

CPSIA information can be obtained
at www.ICGtesting.com
Printed in the USA
BVHW010732030422
632942BV00001B/2

9 781684 339372